nit-
pickin'

For my grandsons, Gideon,
Sky, Silas, and Jasper — N. V. L.

For my kid brother,
James Benton Booth — G. B.

Atheneum Books for Young Readers
An imprint of Simon & Schuster Children's Publishing Division
1230 Avenue of the Americas, New York, New York 10020
Text copyright © 2008 by Nancy Van Laan
Illustrations copyright © 2008 by George Booth
Book design by Ann Bobco
The text for this book is set in Mendoza.
The illustrations for this book are rendered in ballpoint pen on paper, and digitally colored.
Manufactured in China
First Edition
10 9 8 7 6 5 4 3 2 1
Library of Congress Cataloging-in-Publication Data
Van Laan, Nancy.
Nit-pickin' / by Nancy Van Laan; illustrated by George Booth — 1st ed.
p. cm.
Summary: Family members go to great lengths to rid their child of head lice.
ISBN-13: 978-0-689-83898-9
ISBN-10: 0-689-83898-0
[1. Pediculosis—Fiction. 2. Lice—Fiction.] I. Booth, George, 1926– ill. II. Title.
PZ7.V3269 Ni 2002
[E]—dc21
00-062077

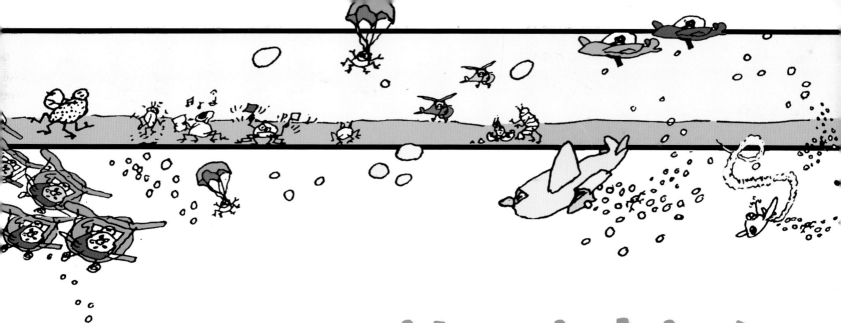

nit-pickin'

nancy van laan and george booth

Atheneum Books for Young Readers • New York London Toronto Sydney

Cooties were a-crawlin'
on my head, on my head,
cooties were a-crawlin'
on my head.

I was scritcha-scratchin'
while a batch-a bugs
was hatchin',
yes, those cooties were
attachin' to my head.

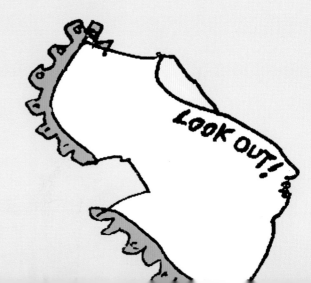

LOOK OUT!

Ma was entertainin'
all the ladies from
the bridge club
while those cooties were
a-crawlin' on my head.

Daddy was a-diggin',
plantin' roses in
the garden
while those cooties were
a-crawlin' on my head.

Gramps was watchin' TV
in the playroom with my sister

while Mama was a-biddin',
and Daddy was a-diggin',
and I was all a-prickly
'cause my hair felt kinda tickly,
fulla creepy-crawlin' cooties
on my head.

Gramma was a-choppin'
yucky collard greens for supper
while those cooties were
a-crawlin' on my head.

She swooped down to catch 'em
when she saw me scritcha-scratchin'.
"There's *bugs* throwin' a picnic
on your head!" she said.
"There's bugs throwin' a picnic
on your head."

Now, Gramma started nittin',
a nitty nit-pickin',
got busy pickin' nits
offa my hair.

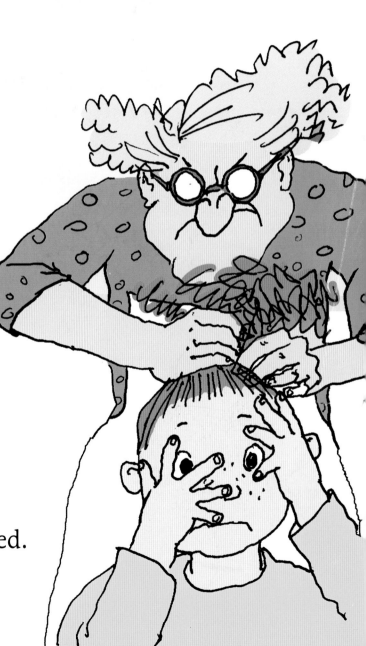

"Eee-youch!" I cried.
"Hold still," Gramma yowled.
"EEOYOW!" I howled.
"Hush yo' mouth!" Gramps growled.

"Now, y'all stop your squigglin',
a-grumblin', and a-wigglin'.
Those itty-bitty nitties
are givin' you the fitties,
so we gotta get 'em out
of your hair."

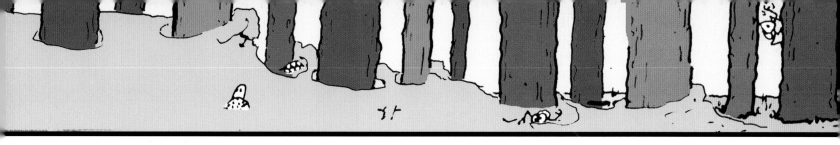

Now Gramma slopped the mayo
on my head, on my head.
Gramma slopped the mayo
on my head.

Sister was a-chucklin'
while I was busy fussin',
"please don't stick me in between
two slices of bread!"

Then Mama started fiddlin'
with somethin' in the kitchen—
that ol' slimy plastic coverin'
she puts around the chicken—
and she wrapped it all around
my sufferin' head.

"Eee-yuk!" I cried.
"Hold still!" Mama growled.
"EEYEW!" I howled.
"Pipe down!" Daddy yowled.

Now Gramps began a-mixin'
and a-brewin' and a-fixin'.
Then he poured some smelly stuff
on my head.

"Ick, gross!" I screamed.
"I been kerosene'd!
  Now y'all get yer lotions
  and yer wrappin's
  and yer potions
  and yer nit-pickin' hands
  outta my hair!"

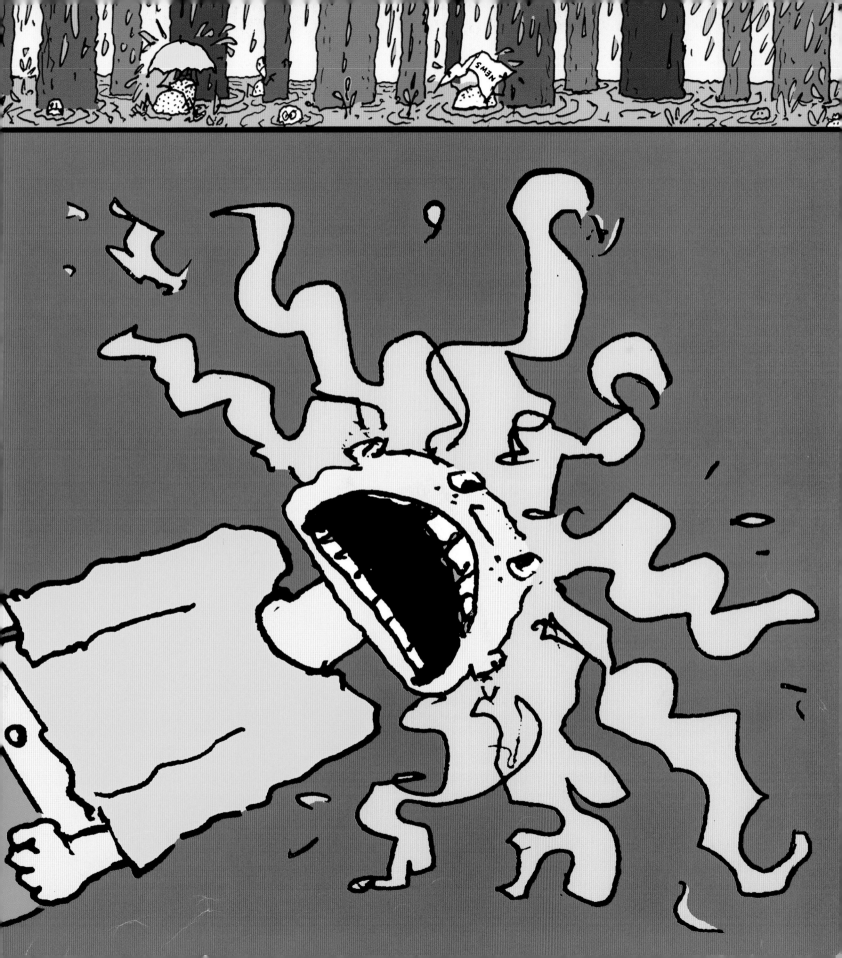

Gramma stopped a-rubbin'.
Daddy stopped a-scrubbin'.
Ma stopped a-wrappin'.

Gramps began a-nappin'.
Sis quit pooh-poohin'.
And I stopped boo-hooin'.

Then I ran to the bathroom
and got busy. . .

. . . shampooin'!

Now, nuthin' is a-crawlin'
on my head, on my head.
Nothin' is a crawlin'
on my head.

There's no more scritcha-scratchin'
'cause no batch-a bugs is hatchin'.
No more cooties and their cousins
are a-crawlin' by the dozens.
No more itty-bitty nitties
are a-throwin' any fitties.

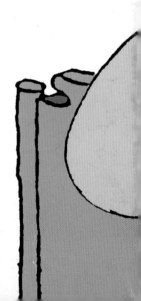

Nope, no cooties are a-crawlin' on my head.